SERGEANT GEORGE AND THE DRAGOON

 # 10   9-10-18

A NIGHT STALKERS 5E ROMANCE STORY

M. L. BUCHMAN

Buchman Bookworks

Other works by M. L. Buchman:

---

*O*ne year minus three days.

Colour Sergeant George Hayman was counting the days, but not for the reasons he had expected. When his commander had told him that he was to be a foreign-military exchange liaison with the Americans of the 160th Night Stalkers 5th Battalion E Company, his protests fell on deaf ears.

"They're the most advanced helicopter company the Yanks have flying, sergeant. Besides, you are one of the very few who has the security clearance they require."

Because of your family connections, he didn't say.

George's father was an unspecified, but *very* highly placed official in MI-6, the foreign intelligence service. It had made Father's life easier for George and Mother to be cleared to SC status or better. It had let Father sit in the parlor with them while reading through his less classified files. George's own work with the Special Forces 7th Squadron RAF had led him to get the DV—Developed Vetting—the UK's highest-level clearance as well.

To this day, Father never spoke about anything he was

working on. Or even precisely who he worked for. It remained rather unclear whether that was due to information compartmentalization or to Father being a taciturn bastard—George felt he was finally getting a good 'handle' on American euphemism after a year minus three days. He favored the latter conclusion.

Either way, his DV clearance meant that he had what the Yanks were after. And his commander had chosen him for the assignment.

"But, sir, they are always so…full of themselves."

"Bottle it, I believe the Americans say."

"I think it's 'Jar it,' sir." (He knew better now.)

"Jar it, then. Cowboys or not, I need to learn what they know. So, gather your hounds and drain your stirrup cup, or whatever you types do."

"Saddle up, sir." He was going to America, after all.

And one-year-minus-three-days ago, he'd landed in the sweltering wilderness of Fort Rucker, Alabama. Such places were fit for neither man nor beast, but they *were* fit for perhaps the finest crew he'd ever served with. He was going to be sorry to go back home. The weather had turned out to not be an issue because the 5E's mission tempo was so high that they were rarely *at* Fort Rucker. Instead they were in places sufficiently awful to make Mother Rucker (as the fort was known) appear actually palatable.

Even stranger, the lead pilot on the *Calamity Jane II*—a huge MH-47G Chinook helicopter—was indeed a cowboy, a real one. Captain Justin Roberts came from a long line of Texas horse breeders and wore his Stetson whenever he wasn't wearing his flight helmet. The others on the crew had come from wildly varied backgrounds—each incredibly impressive in his own way. Or *her* own way.

He'd landed as their starboard-side gunner and second crew chief to Sergeant Carmen Parker. A talkative, funny, and outspoken redhead who knew more about how and why helicopters worked than anyone he'd ever met. Working with her hadn't been a honing of his craft; it had been a Level 8 doctoral program in its own right in both operations and strategy.

And now there were only three days left before his return to the UK.

"Last mission," he meant it for himself, but he still wasn't used to the always-live intercom that this team favored.

"I don't know, gang," Carmen called out. "We gonna miss him?"

He'd finally learned to not be hurt by Carmen's teases, but it had taken a long time to understand that she only teased people she liked—and to them she was merciless.

A chorus of "Nah!" "Nope!" and "Not a chance!" sounded over the headphones in his helmet.

"Right back to you, you undeserving lot." They were the most deserving team he'd ever met. A Brit nuanced their feelings. The Americans were possessed of no nuance at all. Their use of a single emphatic word, where five would do nicely, made it terribly difficult to isolate sarcasm from forthright intent.

Carmen sounded a loud raspberry, telling him that he'd managed to get the hang of it well enough before he left—if not by much.

"Try not to screw us up on your last flight, mate," Carmen called out as they swung down for the second extraction of the night.

'Mate' was Strine from Down Under, not British. He had attempted to correct that on his second day—and his third and fourth. It turned out to be something Carmen had apparently already known and all of his protests had only served to embed it deeply in her repertoire.

Their first recovery tonight had happened quietly—a

single Delta Force recon specialist had strolled out of the Colombian jungle at twilight and stepped onto the helicopter's lowered rear ramp before it even touched the ground. He'd worn full jungle camo and enough gear on his massive frame to intimidate anyone. *Solo* recon. The Delta operators were even crazier than the SAS he normally carried around back home.

The second extraction was occurring at a cliff edge over a fast-running river after night had fallen. The jungle itself was a hundred meters back, but there was no clear spot to set down atop the cliff edge. So, they were forced to hover *beyond* the cliff edge. As the helo swung into position—tail ramp touching the stone and the long body of the helo hovering a hundred feet above the river—the jungle roared to life.

Not just monkeys and parrots and whatever other denizens resided there. Rather, the trees were suddenly alive with more muzzle flashes than he could count. He hit the power switch on his M134D minigun, grabbed onto the twin handles—

And was thrown down to the steel deck—*hard!*

For a second he didn't know what had hit him. The gun was driven by an electric motor, but the jolt hadn't come through his hands. Then he understood the problem. Despite the helo's armor at his position, and the large weapon sitting in the middle of the small window, a stray round had found a gap and drilled into his arm.

OMG but he understood the problem!

His upper arm had been punched by no teasing blow of Carmen knuckling the triceps nerve cluster.

This was a hammer of pain that no training instructor had ever handed out. The big Delta guy strolled up to him and squatted as if he was inspecting a mosquito bite.

"Huh," he wrapped a bandage around it which caused

George to blank for a second as the pain slammed in double-fold. He came to as the Delta finished putting George's arm in a sling. He was leaning against the side of the hull now, out of everyone's way.

"Better have someone look at that when you get back to base."

"Ruddy hell yeah!" Did the guy think he was going to just walk around with it until some fairy godmother magically healed it? Or had that been more backward American under-statement?

Then the guy stepped up to the minigun and took over firing it.

George shoved his visor out of his way. When he'd been hurled back, he must have become disconnected from the umbilical that projected data on the inside of his visor. With it out of the way, he now lay in the cargo bay, surreally awash with the dim red of night operations lighting.

Digging one-handed into his own medkit, George found a fentanyl lollipop. It looked more like a white multi-vitamin on a stick. Once he managed to get it out of its foil pack—never meant to be done one-handed with a hand shaking from the pain—and tucked into his cheek, the pain backed off.

Way off! No wonder there were all the training warnings about how addictive these things were. A shot of morphine both punched the pain and punched you under. This felt great. It almost convinced him that he could stand up and do a little fighting himself, though the Delta seemed to be doing a 'bang-up' job by the sound of it.

George slouched against the inside of the helo and listened to the buzz-saw roar of the minigun lashing out four thousand rounds per minute in two- and three-second bursts.

One. Two. Three.

The guy shifted angles.

One. Two.

He didn't quite have the waltz beat that George had found useful to hum while firing, but he was close enough. Short, sharp, focused firing was the trick.

One. Two. *Clank!*

Clank? That wasn't a good sound. He looked up to see the guy testing the barrel spin. That looked normal, but the ammunition belt wasn't moving.

"Sounds like you sheared the pin in the delinker. Two-dollar part, but takes ten minutes to replace it." He was pretty impressed that he could put those thoughts together. The fentanyl was definitely doing its job—he felt light, as if he might start floating.

"We've got, like, thirty seconds," the guy whinged.

George shrugged his indifference—then wished like hell he hadn't. The fentanyl was good, but the pain from the ill-considered movement slammed in hard and his vision tunneled badly.

For a time, there were just intermittent flashes of consciousness.

A military MRZR all-terrain vehicle with four soldiers aboard racing up the rear ramp.

Some shouting.

A body dumped across his lower legs.

The MRZR and the Delta gone.

More shouting.

None of it from the body lying on him.

No blood on their back.

Being careful of his arm, he rolled the soldier over so that now he was lying across George's thighs instead of his calves. He landed with a groan of life.

Definitely blood on the front, the trousers were soaked in blood—which showed up as black beneath the helo's red light. And the soldier was clearly awake and in intense pain—eyes squeezed shut hard and teeth gritted.

The female soldier.

Unable to face the challenge of his med kit again, he pulled the fentanyl lollipop out of his mouth and stuck it in hers.

He definitely missed it as he began basic triage even if logic said that it couldn't wear off that fast. It certainly felt as if it did.

Her leg was wrong. Very wrong.

"Medic!" he shouted, but no one appeared to be listening. Carmen was still manning the other minigun. Another was wielding a fire extinguisher at something. The last soldier was still looking out the rear ramp where the MRZR had disappeared into the night. The only other person in the cargo bay was lying against the far side of the hull—with his eyes open and his jaw slack. Bad sign. Very bad.

The woman in his lap fainted and her face relaxed. Not much to see beneath the camouflage battle paint. He checked, she still had a pulse. Apparently it was up to him to keep that going.

Him, the one-armed man.

One year minus three days.

Go figure! (He was fairly sure that he had that idiom right.)

_____

2

*M*arta Proulx came to with a tasteless lollipop in her mouth. She'd always been partial to *sucette—citron* was her favorite. She loved anything lemon. Her mother's lemon tarts were the best of any French pastry shop. This *sucette* had nothing to like about it, but she couldn't find the energy to spit it out.

A man was tugging at her clothes.

She hit him.

Or tried to.

She felt as weak as a kitten and barely managed to hit him at all.

He shrieked as if she'd run him down with a her Peugeot.

"Do not do that ever again," the man glared down at her. His accent was very British. Posh British.

"Then stop, *monsieur,* with the taking off of my clothes." Somewhere in there was a coherent sentence.

"I will if you agree to stop bleeding."

"I'm bleeding?" She shouldn't be bleeding. Then she remembered the race through the jungle. Hostiles sprouting up faster than the foliage—which was definitely saying a lot.

Most of her career had been in Southwest Asian deserts. The incredible bio-density of South American jungles still startled her every time, even though she'd been here for six months.

"Bleeding copiously," the Brit observed.

"Well…" she tried to connect the thought to something, but it was a hard struggle. "Make it stop."

"Hence, the removal of your clothes," he waved a pair of shears at her.

"Oh. Cut away."

The gun battle that she could only vaguely recall faded away. The few crew members in the cargo bay were rushing about as if their was a great cause for alarm, but Marta was having trouble concentrating enough to see what it was.

To block them out, she closed her eyes and tried to imagine that it was a cool spring day back home in Chartres. Sitting out on the cobbled square with a treat from *La Chocolaterie* on the Place du Cygne. The sun warm, the tourists to the Chartres gothic cathedral not yet thick as flies…

Each tug on her trousers destroyed the image with fresh jolts of pain.

"Be careful, you cocky swine." She'd served with enough Brits to know what they all were.

"You French are always whinging. I'm doing the best I can one-handed."

"Then use two hands, fool." That's when she noticed he had one arm in a sling and was sweating badly. More than might be called for by the jungle's heat. Actually, he shouldn't be sweating at all; there was a pleasant draft flowing through the helicopter.

The helicopter?

Unsure of how she came to be here, she looked around.

"Where's the rest of the crew?" It seemed there should be more people here. No sign of Tanya, her team leader.

Somehow she'd driven through hell to get them here, but where was she now?

The Brit waved his shears across the helo. Barely visible beneath the red nightlights she stared into Carl's blank face. He lay crumpled against the other side of the hull and didn't look as if he'd be moving again except into a body bag. She closed her eyes, not wanting to see more.

"It's not going well, is it?" She asked but kept her eyes tightly closed.

"I don't know. The wound looks clean, just bloody. Can you raise your knee?" With his assistance, she managed to, and thanks to the fentanyl, managed to do it without shrieking like a schoolgirl. Even as a schoolgirl she'd never been the sort to shriek.

"Marta has displayed a fine attention to her studies. However, she is not a team player—she strives to be the best, which is not very humble. Worse, she does so, uncaring of the cost to everyone around her." Sister Mary Patrick had sounded almost gleeful in reporting the fault to her mother.

Sister Mary Patrick was wrong. Marta was a fine team player, once she found a team worth playing for like—

"Ahh!"

"What?"

"My leg, it is not supposed to have a hole in it." She should have kept her eyes closed. By propping her knee up, he'd been able to cut away the rest of the material around her thigh. And now she could see where the round had sliced through. It wasn't arterial bleeding or she'd be dead, but it was very bloody.

"At least yours was a meat shot. I think I lost a section of bone." He spread a small line of superglue on the bullet hole, then squeezed the edges together. He groaned as he twisted around to glue what must be the exit hole on the back of her thigh.

11

She tried to close her eyes, but couldn't help watching. Despite his injuries, he was gentle.

"Bloody hell!"

"What?"

"Nothing," he said too quickly.

"*What?*" Was the sudden chill of the breeze over the steel deck just imagined, or was it from soon-to-be-terminal blood loss and shock?

"I just glued my sling to your thigh."

He began to remove the sling and she could see the agony across his features. Even if he was a Brit, no one deserved that.

She held out the fentanyl lollipop and tucked it into his mouth the next time he groaned.

He finally managed to extract his arm from the sling and sit upright once more.

He dug into her medkit which she wore over her stomach. It actually tickled a little despite her armored vest between them. He pulled out a triangular bandage and fashioned a second sling.

"You know…" She reached out to help him settle it in place.

"What?" His breath was still a hiss as they got his arm settled.

"You had a pair of shears."

"You're suggesting perhaps that I would have been better served had I snipped your leg off? In retrospect, I'm inclined to agree."

"No. But you might have snipped off the corner of the sling."

"Huh!" His grunt sounded very American. He pulled out the fentanyl lollipop and inspected it carefully.

After exchanging a woeful glance, he chucked it up into

the airflow and it whipped out the rear ramp of the racing helo and into the night.

"Blast," he sighed as he cradled his arm and leaned back against the helo's vibrating hull.

The last thing Marta recalled was lying in the Brit's lap as exhaustion, fentanyl, and blood loss finally combined to take her under.

e opened his eyes.
White.

Lots and lots of white.

It started at George's shoulder. Blinking hard to bring it into focus, he managed to follow the line of it all of the way to his fingertips. Those stuck out the end of the fiberglass cast that dangled from a sling above him.

Would they wiggle?

Did he want to know if they didn't?

Taking a deep breath, he tried. They did. Everything from shoulder to wrist was a land of numb, but he could wiggle his fingers and feel the round edges of the cast. Victory!

Everything else was white as well. The ceiling, the walls, the sheets.

Hospital white.

Uh-oh.

So *not* a good sign. (*Nailed the idiom,* some thought reported through the fog that seemed to wrap around him. Or should it have been: *So* not a good sign? With an elongated 'o'? Whatever. *Oh god, another idiom. Shut up!*)

Then he refocused on the cast on his arm. Perhaps being in hospital made a modicum of sense.

The bed beside his was white as well, except for the woman lying atop the covers. She was the only color in the room—fantastically so. Long brunette hair that ruffled over her pillow (white) with chocolate brown eyes to match. Her face sported the lovely high cheekbones and full lips of the French.

"Bon matin!"

Ha! He had nuked it…nailed it. One of those things.

She *was* French.

"Good morning…I suppose." George blinked again and saw more white—this time her gauze-wrapped leg stretched across the sheet (more white). "Oh! It's you. The woman with the leg."

"Well, I was thinking hard about transforming into someone else—someone who hadn't been shot—but that hasn't been working very well for me. It's the first time anyone has recognized me by my legs."

"They're nice legs." He must still be drugged to utter such a remark. But they were. She looked splendidly long and lovely stretched out atop the covers in her hospital gown. He appreciated the lack of length in the gown's hem.

"They were nicer before they were shot twice."

"Twice?" He tried to jolt upright. The painkiller kept the pain at bay, but the cast extended up onto his shoulder and it weighted him into place.

"Calme," she instructed in the wonderful accent of hers.

"Where else were you hit?" The horror that he might have left her to bleed to death because he hadn't checked for other wounds was overwhelming.

"Nowhere else. Once I was shot from in front and once I was shot from behind. Two separate damage paths, which is why there was so much blood. You…saved my life."

"My pleasure, ma'am. You don't exactly sound pleased."

"I don't enjoy being beholden to any man."

"Perhaps if I were a woman."

That earned him a light laugh that sounded even more French than her lovely accent. "It does not go well with your three-day growth of beard. Which looks good on you, by the way."

"My what?" He rubbed his chin, and it was definitely there. "Three days?"

"We both spent the day after the mission in surgery. We're in an Aruban hospital, by the way—the closest Western hospital to our extraction point. Yours was rather more drastic, they had to remove a section of bone and replace it with a titanium rod."

He did note that neither of them were on life monitors or IV drips which he supposed practically made them outpatients. A good sign.

"You slept through yesterday."

George could only stare at the ceiling in shock. This was now the third day since his injury, which meant that his year with the Night Stalkers was over. He was going to miss them horribly.

"I'm done."

4

"No you aren't!" Marta was startled by his defeatist tone. "The doctors expect a full recovery." The damage to her own leg was almost as severe. Her bones hadn't been broken, but the bullets had tumbled and ripped up tendon and muscle badly. But no one was going to stop her from getting back into the battle.

"No, I mean I'm done here."

"You're quitting? You qualified to fly on a Night Stalkers helicopter and you're quitting because you were shot. What did you think Special Operations was? A child's game? Stupid British fool. Yes, I called you a fool before and I was right to do so."

She could hear that she was unleashing *la tempête de Marta* as the nuns had called the storm of her temper, but it was something she'd never managed to truly control. Especially not when someone was being so foolish.

Yes, she had been a poor team player in Catholic school. That was only because she hadn't found a truly superior team until she'd joined the 13th Parachute Dragoons.

"Hey, uh… What's your name anyway?"

"I am not telling some British quitter." Never. Neither hot pincers nor bad pastries would—

"I'm not quitting, whoever you are." His tone was sharp. Especially sharp considering that he was British. That made it especially cutting—roughly the same level as the French sniff of disdain.

"But you just said— Foof!" She wiggled her fingers at him in dismissal and give him the disdainful sniff. "Now you are a liar."

"No. Now I am once again a member of the No. 7 Squadron in Her Majesty's Royal Air Force."

"I thought you were a Night Stalker."

"A one-year exchange. Which ends today. I'm done."

"Is that what you meant?"

He nodded solemnly.

"*Un moment.* The 7th Squadron?"

"Yes, I'm a helo crew chief for Chinook helicopters."

"No, you aren't. You fly for Joint Special Forces. They're the very best of the UK. And you just spent a year flying with the Night Stalkers?" Now that was a man who definitely would play at the same level she did.

He offered only a tight nod.

"I'm just finishing six months with an inter-force recon team. I'm with the 13th." And now she would see if he really was who he said he was, by how he responded. If he gave her the standard "You're kidding, right?", she was going to punch his arm again—much harder now that she wasn't dying from blood loss.

His low whistle of surprise said he knew what it was. "The 13th *Régiment de Dragons Parachutistes.*" He even managed the pronunciation reasonably well and knew that dragoon in French was *dragon*.

She had fought so hard to make it into the dragoon regiment of France's Spec Ops. No one understood how hard it

SERGEANT GEORGE AND THE DRAGOON

was. Not the Catholic sisters, not her mother, not any of the regular military she met. Not even the men who had applied and failed. They would brag to her about their failed attempts as if it was the high point of their lives—as if she would ever accept a lover who had failed.

"No wonder you want to be beholden to no man—or woman with a three-day beard."

Curiously, she believed that *he* understood how hard she'd fought to reach her goal.

5

George faded out before he learned her name.

He faded back in for doctors and once more for food, both of which she slept through. They, or their drugs, were badly out of sync.

Which was too bad. Because now it was two in the morning and he was wide awake with only the soft rattle of the air conditioning to keep him company.

He had learned so much over the last year to take back to his home unit. Carmen had taught him shortcuts that weren't shortcuts, they were just ten times more efficient than how the manual said to perform a task. Captain Roberts and Danny Corvo, his copilot, had obliged him with well-considered answers to his endless questions. Their innovations in overlapping minigun coverage and infiltration techniques were going to shake up some of the 'good old boys' back home.

And the lovely woman from the 13th dragoons of France had captivated his thoughts. Special Operations women were a rare commodity in any country's military. It wasn't for lack of need; rather, in his opinion, most women lacked a certain bloody-mindedness. Carmen had been a prime example of what he'd always thought was needed for a woman to succeed in Spec Ops—her attitude was as rough-and-tough as any male's, maybe more than most. Yet, no matter how she might act, Carmen was also the core of the team as much or more than its captain. Women brought a cohesiveness that a mere 'band of brothers' often lacked.

The woman lying beside him had that steel core—and a matching spark of temper. But she was so very purely female. Perhaps it was because she was French—

The woman lying *beside* him?

"How did we end up in the same room?" He asked the darkness.

"I have been wondering that myself," the darkness answered.

"You're awake?" He could feel the weight of her scoff at his inane question.

"I think it is because I was lying in your lap when I passed out—which was *after* you passed out." Apparently everything was a competition for her.

"Carmen." It had to be.

"Carmen? Is that the name of your lover?"

"No. It's the name of my fellow crew chief on the Night Stalkers' helo. It is exactly the sort of thing she would do to 'mess' with me: see us lying together and tell the med team we were a couple."

"It sounds like something a former lover would do to make you uncomfortable. Is she very sexy, this Carmen? All dark and Spanish?"

"Yes. No. She—" George let out an exasperated breath. "Carmen is redheaded, very American. Yes, very sexy. And no, she was never my lover."

"Is something wrong with you?"

"Yes, I'm missing part of my arm."

"I mean with you not taking this sexy redheaded Carmen as a lover."

"She is also married to the helo's copilot." Another strangeness to the Night Stalkers 5E. Their company was some sort of experiment where couples were allowed to fly together—which worked amazingly well in his estimation. It was so unusual, that he wasn't even sure if he should mention it to his commander when he returned to the 7th Squadron. Or if he'd be believed.

"Oh," was all the woman lying near him in the dark said. No surprise, merely acknowledgement. She was French, freer with the whole 'lover' concept, so perhaps that explained it.

He contemplated different British ways to present it. Maybe it was something that could only work in America.

Before he could ask for her thoughts, he heard the woman's breathing shift back into sleep. He wasn't far behind her.

6

"Two weeks' convalescence." Marta balanced on her crutches and blinked at the brilliant Aruban sunshine from beneath the shaded entrance of the hospital. The sun that had come in through their room's window had seemed so inviting. Out here, it was a blinding affront.

"Did you opt for home or the hotel?"

They had offered them the option. No more willing to explain herself to Mother than to anyone else, she'd opted to stay in Aruba. She held up the room key they'd issued her.

The Brit held up a room key as well. Thankfully with a different number.

But later that evening, as she sat alone and wondered what to do with herself—Aruba television broadcast mostly in Dutch—a knock sounded on her door.

"I'm not much of a cook one-handed," he had greeted her.

"I'm not much of a cook at all." Thankfully, he made no wisecrack about French women who couldn't cook. She had heard it a thousand-and-one times, about a thousand beyond her tolerance level.

"I'll buy you dinner."

And just that simply, it had set the pattern. Physical therapy in the mornings, lunch by the hotel's pool, afternoons chatting quietly over bizarre tropical drinks in the shade of a thatched hut by the turquoise sea, and dinner in a different restaurant each night.

For three days they had declared that the six hundred years of Anglo-French wars had not ended with Napoleon's defeat in 1815. Though her companion had preferred to argue it began even two centuries earlier, as his people had fought in the Battle of Hastings in 1066, but that seemed a rather trite point to her.

To pass the time, they had decided to break any cross-channel armistice and resume hostile competition while here on the Aruban beaches—each fought hard to convince the other of the places they must visit. By the end of their "battle" she had a list of places in the British countryside that sounded lovely and he had a list of French restaurants to try from Chartres to Bordeaux.

Over the days, his interest in American idiom had turned to French idiom—which would have been easier to explain if he spoke any French. But he was a wise man. He had pursued it especially during physical therapy sessions which had been a very welcome distraction.

The first time they made love had almost been inevitable. She'd had a particularly tough physical therapy session that day and couldn't find the energy to leave the room. Being the noble, one-armed gentleman that he had proved himself to be, he had gone out to a local Bavarian restaurant and returned with beer-and-cheese soup, chicken schnitzel, and Black Forest cake. Maybe it was the tiered layers of rich, dark chocolate that had caused her to succumb. Perhaps it was how long she'd been without a man—she chose her lovers carefully and rarely.

He had risen to clear the table and she had pulled him back down for a chocolate-rich kiss. He might be one-handed and she one-legged, but the results were spectacular.

It became a regular part of their therapy. Practiced happily at rising in the morning, going to bed at night, and more rather than less often with a meal.

He was a gentle lover, something new in her experience. And very, very inventive.

"I thought you were British."

"That does not imply a lack of interest in sex. I simply don't brag about it to every person I meet. Though you offer a great deal to brag about, fair lady."

And there it was again. For reasons that eluded her, after waking up together in the same hospital room as a couple, they had never introduced themselves by name. At first it had felt awkward, *I almost died in your lap, but I don't know your name.*

Then during the "declared war" it had become a point of honor to ask nothing of their past, including their name. After the war, but before the sex, they had talked of past and family in ways she never had before. The sole offspring of an unwed mother who was also devoutly Catholic and had seen her daughter as both a sin and a blessing—and constant evidence of her own failings. He, the renegade son who had dropped out of Oxford to enter the military rather than pursuing a posting to the foreign office.

Somehow, revealing so much of her past had been easier without having a name. She was able to speak of herself as if she was someone else. How she had spent her entire life trying to prove herself to others because she could never do so to her mother. Or herself. The impossibly deep answers drew them together in such unexpected ways until she felt closer to him than she had with any other—man or woman.

And now, having a nameless lover, had allowed them to

discuss past lovers and past failures with equal anonymity. It also added a spice that neither of them appeared interested in losing.

7

The taxi to Queen Beatrix International Airport was desperately silent and George didn't know how to break it.

"We French are pragmatists."

The relief was so great that George almost cried out when she spoke. "I don't want to be pragmatic, practical, or any other p-word about you."

"We French have no choice but to be that way, with our country trapped between Germany, Italy, and Spain."

"Not to mention occasional British incursions." He couldn't help reminding her. They traded brief smiles about their "war" as the lovely Aruba seaside slid by wholly unattended.

"Some of those incursions were most enjoyable." And her smile was brighter at the memory of the lovemaking.

For that's what it had been. Sex between two injured soldiers had become lovemaking. Last night, knowing it was their last, every gesture had seemed so full of meaning that not a single word had been spoken. That had to be what

31

making love felt like, for he'd never experienced anything else like it.

"There are vacations, the occasional leave..." the joy disappeared from her voice as she listed the options he too had thought of.

"We could both run off and join the French Foreign Legion."

It was understood that neither of them were willing to leave their service. Unable to say anything else, they simply clung to each other for the long thirteen-hour transit from Aruba to Heathrow via Miami. She had a medical upgrade to First Class for her leg, and he had simply paid for it out of pocket—half a month's pay, but worth every farthing.

She laid over with him for two days in London at his parents' townhouse.

Mother had fussed and Father had simply watched them as unreadably as ever.

8

*M*arta wasn't happy with feeling like a bug targeted by a rifle's laser-red sighting pointer. The townhouse was even more posh than their accents—a far cry from the flat above Mama's pastry shop. Marta also wasn't happy that she'd finally had to give up her first name to meet his parents.

They were Marta and George now. It took something away from them that she couldn't identify. She wanted it back, that cloak of anonymity that she had worn for two wonderful weeks. Names made something already terribly important, even more so.

With George's mother saying, "Marta this…" and "Marta that…" she felt cornered by the simple kindness of a fine hostess.

Alone together in George's room, neither of them used the other's name—not once—but it was only the slightest of respites. The end hung like doom itself on her plane ticket and the orders calling for her to report in.

It was their last day together. "Her Brit" had fallen back asleep after their morning loving and she had crept out in search of coffee and a sweet roll. The house seemed echoingly silent so she tip-toed into the kitchen as quietly as she could with her cane, and spoiled all of her efforts with a yelp of surprise.

George Senior sat at the small walnut kitchen table in the steel-and-granite kitchen with a newspaper, but he was watching her. He had the same dark eyes as his son. And the same burning intelligence.

Marta offered a careful greeting smile, poured her coffee, but was unsure what to do next.

He nodded to the seat opposite him so, at a loss, she sat down as normally as she could manage—then dropped her cane so loudly on the floor that she almost jumped out of her skin.

"You are clearly in the same line of work as my son. Both wounded at the same time, on an international mission together that ended in Aruba."

She startled. How much did this stern, closed man know about his son's duties—which were supposed to be secret? Then she recalled that the tags on their luggage would have given that much away. So, she nodded and sipped her coffee.

"I have never seen him both so happy and so sad at the same time."

"It's like an ache in the chest that will never go away." That didn't sound like the Marta she knew, but it was true.

He folded his paper neatly and set it aside before looking her directly in the eye. It seemed that he was the darker version of his son. His coloring was much the same, but George's easy smile was lacking.

"I'm not very pleased with the concept of my son and daughter-in-law living in harm's way."

"Daughter-in law? We're not—" But his unflinching gaze said that he knew things she hadn't dared hope for. Or even think about. The image of the two of them together had so haunted her waking thoughts that it had moved into her dreams.

Married to George? She could think of no other she'd prefer…ever!

"We're soldiers, your son and I." It was something no civilian could truly understand. "We joined to serve. We both entered Special Forces because we wanted to make the greatest impact possible with our lives." It was one of the things she'd come to most respect in George. She had dismissed him for "being done" but had since learned there couldn't be a thought further from his mind. He had become as committed to the Night Stalkers as he had to his own unit and he felt the pain of loyalty.

"You were both on inter-force exchange programs." George's father didn't make it a question.

"Different ones that happened to coincide at the wrong moment. Or perhaps the best moment, because he saved my life."

George Senior gathered up his newspaper and his coffee cup and moved to the sink to rinse it out.

She glanced down and saw a blue file remained on the table. It had no markings but a code number on the tab. "Sir, you left behind a file."

He looked right at her across the length of the kitchen. "I don't know what you're talking about. I *always* know exactly where all of my classified documents are." Then he left the room.

She heard the front door open, then close as he greeted his driver.

Very slowly, she turned the file to face her. His intent was clear, but still her hands were shaking as she, feeling as if she was risking her life yet again, opened the file.

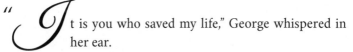

9

"It is you who saved my life," George whispered in her ear.

"How do you figure that?"

"Without you, my heart would never have known what it was missing."

"Perhaps it was your father, George Senior, who saved us both."

George still couldn't believe that. Somehow Marta had won Father over just as she had conquered himself. (France 2. Britain 0. He really must get back in the game.)

He held her hand tightly as they crossed the carpark and joined the loose queue of people heading into "The Doughnut." The circular Government Communications Headquarters was indeed shaped like the massive American doughnut lying on its side. He was going to work inside an American idiom.

The agency Father had never spoken of in all of his years was Five Eyes. It was an intelligence sharing organization that included: the Brits (the UK, along with Australia, New Zealand, and Canada) and the Yanks.

Another organization, Nine Eyes, ran by slightly different rules but with a similar purpose. It added on Denmark, Norway, the Netherlands, and—thank all the powers-that-be —France. The operation had been overjoyed at the addition of two fully cleared, field-trained operatives with experience embedding within their allies' forces.

"I have just one question," he leaned in to whisper in her ear.

"Yes?" Her voice was pure, lush tease.

"What is your last name? The wedding is this weekend and I think I should know my wife's last name before I marry her."

"You didn't read the invitations?"

"That rather seemed like cheating."

Marta stopped him by their joined hands, turned into his arms, and kissed him so thoroughly that reporting to their new job fell several places on his priority list. It also earned him a severe throat clearing from Father who he'd forgotten was walking in the crowd close behind them.

"Proulx," his father said, and moved on ahead of them. "It means Valiant."

"Valiant," George whispered. "Of course you saved my life."

"Sergeant George slayed the heart of the French dragoon," she murmured into his ear as he held her.

"And as a reward, he won the heart of the princess."

"He did."

She sighed happily in his arms one last time before they turned hand-in-hand and—just like in her dream—walked forward together.

IF YOU ENJOYED THIS, YOU'RE
GONNA LOVE:

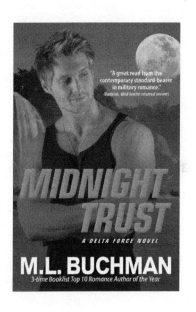

*I*t wasn't his sniper rifle, but Chad could easily be talked into having an M134D minigun of his own to play with now and then.

He short-bursted just two to three seconds at a time—which at four thousand rounds per minute was a daunting couple hundred rounds each time he hit the trigger. When he was on the hustle with his combat rifle, he might shoot a round or two per second. With his sniper rifle, he only ever had to fire it once per target. The minigun might not hit with every round the way he did—Delta Force training wasn't about wasting ammunition—but...

"Hoo-ee doggies! Just lay down now, dudes. Daddy's got a brand new toy."

"Easy hotshot," Carmen, the way-cute redhead on the big Chinook helicopter's other gun practically laughed.

"Suppressive fire. That's what I'm talking about! Suppressive, hell. This thing is a shredder."

The twin-rotor helicopter was making its second pickup of the night.

He'd been the first: out doing solo recon deep in the

Colombian jungle. Just before sunset the Night Stalkers' M47G helo had swooped in, he'd strolled up the rear ramp, and twenty tons of twin-rotor helo had flitted away with no one the wiser. A couple of other helos had circled high above on guard duty, but weren't needed.

Their second pickup—in the last of the failing dusk—wasn't going so hot. Masses of groundfire ripped through the humid, cloying air. One of the joys of the jungle, a man got wetter just standing still than he did running around in most other places.

On the "even worse" side of the list, the Chinook's starboard gunner had just taken a hit right through the gunner's window. It had to be pure luck—put enough lead in the air and you're bound to hit something—their current enemy's rather boring tactic. Had to be, because none of these cocaine-running Colombian hillbillies could shoot that well on purpose.

No fountains of blood sprouted from the gunner's upper arm, which meant the dude's arteries were still flowing in the right direction. Chad had slapped a compression badge on the arm, then tossed it in a sling when it was clear that the bone had been shattered. "Better have someone look at that when you get back to base."

"Ruddy hell *yeah!*" The guy agreed weakly with a posh British accent.

Then Chad had stepped up to the swivel-mounted, six-barrel Gatling minigun himself and patched into the intercom before giving it a try.

Su-weet!

He'd never fired an M134D except during weapons familiarization on the Fort Bragg range—certainly not from the vantage of a hovering helo. This weapon delivered a whole new level of hurt to the bad guys.

The extract being run by the 160th Night Stalkers was a

textbook setup. Hover at the edge of a steep canyon with sixty feet and ten tons of monster, twin-rotor helo hanging over a whole lot of nothing. Lower the three-meter wide rear ramp onto the edge of the cliff, and wait for the cavalry to come trotting out of the jungle. Just to add some spice, the pilots were facing out over the canyon and couldn't see shit behind them, but they were Night Stalkers and had it nailed.

Pure textbook.

Except just like all such scenarios, Chad knew full well *why* they ended up in textbooks...because they always went wrong. This time proved to be no exception.

The jungle ended a hundred meters away, except for just a few scattered trees. Those had forced the helo to hover out at the cliff edge to avoid catching a rotor blade on some wax palm or giant mahogany with helo-crashing in mind.

The good guys had appeared at one end of the clearing while the bad guys were shooting madly from the other.

And from the side.

And from behind the friendlies—which was very unfriendly of them.

Normally an MH-47G Chinook didn't fight—it was the cargo van of Special Operations Forces. They left the dirty work up to the big hammer of the Black Hawks. Except there was so much going on tonight, the two Hawks they'd brought with them were too busy to defend the Chinook as well.

So, Chad leaned out as far as the gun would go and blasted showers of lead back into the jungle's verge. The minigun did a good job of making would-be shooters keep their heads down. Thankfully, these guys weren't exactly quick learners and he kept picking them off in groups of two and three.

"If I was on the other end of this, I'd be diggin' a hole."

"Wouldn't stop me from finding you," Carmen called back

as she too blasted away. She wore a ring, but maybe it was one of those phony "Keep Away" signs that a guy could sometimes talk his way around.

"I dunno. When I dig down, I go *deep*."

Didn't earn him the right kind of laugh, so maybe the ring was real.

He picked off someone with a heavy machine gun and his ammo monkey. Good to have that out of play. The 5.56 mm ammo was a pain—all most of these guys were throwing. But the .50 cal stuff could really hurt—punching holes in people and helicopters—until it suddenly wasn't anymore because he'd blasted it out of existence.

The friendlies were approaching in an MRZR. The four-person military ATV was fast, but not fast enough—they were getting hammered on the long crossing through the sparse trees.

Chad went to unleash his new toy on another section of the unfriendly types.

Pull trigger. Electric motor spins the barrels up to seven hundred RPM, and it starts throwing an impressive line of 7.62 mm rounds into the night. Every fifth one a tracer that shows up brilliant green in his night-vision goggles. It was the strange half-light at end of day where his NVGs were better than nothing, but not by much.

Might as well be firing blind.

For half a second, sweep right.

At a full second, shift and sweep left.

Second and a half—a hellacious grinding noise from the machine and the ammunition belt just stopped moving. The barrels still spun, but the comforting buzz-saw roar of sixty-six supersonic rounds per second wasn't happening.

He let the electric motor spin down.

When he grabbed the barrels and gave them a test spin,

they moved just fine. Hot as hell, but he wore gloves, so it was okay. Hot barrels was normal on a minigun.

He looked down at the wounded Brit leaning with his back against the hull.

"Sounds like you sheared the pin in the delinker. Two-dollar part, but takes ten minutes to replace it."

"We've got like thirty seconds."

The guy shrugged, and even in the NVGs, Chad could see him wince at the pain in his arm.

"Got a jam here. Starboard side. Not clearable," Chad reported over the intercom.

"Shit!" Carmen was not happy. "Damn Delta Force operator comes aboard and breaks my hundred thousand-dollar weapon system."

"This 'damn Delta Force operator' didn't do it to you out of spite."

"Like I'm gonna believe that shit." Too bad she was taken —woman had a mouth on her and kept her sense of humor even when things got bad.

Without comment, The pilots twisted the big helo on its tail. They kept the ramp on the ground and rotated the nose around until Carmen's weapon had almost a full sweep of the jungle, which meant she had to work twice as hard.

"You guys are so damn good," he called out to the pilots as he unlimbered his HK416 rifle. Twenty-round magazine and he only had two spares on him. He'd just gone from a loaded four-thousand round kicker-case bolted to the deck...to sixty.

As the view on his side was now over the night-shrouded canyon, he strode over to join Carmen. Maybe he could get some shots out the edge of her gun window.

He was halfway across the eight-foot-wide cargo bay when it hit him.

Literally.

The MRZR raced aboard, shot up the length of the cargo bay—and slammed into him.

He heard a scream and a curse, but he wasn't sure which one was his as he was thrown forward.

Chad landed on his back between the two pilot seats and his helmet smacked hard against the main console.

"Nice one, cowboy." Captain Roberts looked down at him. "You just shattered our central screen with your head. Haven't you broken enough already?"

"Guess not," Chad managed to admit and wondered about his own body. Was he in shock? He wasn't feeling any pain. Had his body armor saved him…or not? Experience had told him that if he was hurt, he would be feeling it soon enough.

"Well, it's not getting any better. They just knocked out one of our engines." While Roberts flew, the copilot's hands were moving fast. First he pulled the engine fire T-handle and then did more of whatever it was helo copilots did during a crisis.

Chad lay on the radio console that ran between the pilot seats and wondered if he should try getting up. It seemed as if perhaps he should.

He raised his head first. Good sign, his neck still worked.

He could see his left foot was caught between the MRZR's bull-bar bumper and its winch.

He could feel his foot! Another good sign, implying that his spine had remained intact. Attempting to twist his foot free transmitted loud and clear that there was nothing wrong with the nerves in his knee. *Ow!*

The driver was looking at him in some surprise.

Even dressed like a Spec Ops solider—in armored vest, helmet, and enough weaponry to suppress a riot—couldn't hide that the driver was seriously female.

Woman drivers.

THE MRZR'S brakes had worked before Tanya had entered the battle, but she hadn't used them much since then.

Either they were shot out on the crossing or her impact with the side of the Chinook's rear ramp had killed them. The helicopter had twisted just as she'd been racing for the ramp, wanting nothing more than out of the hellhole they'd entered.

At least two of her team were injured—one had nearly blown out her eardrum with a scream as the MRZR slammed to a halt.

Worse, their jungle target had been a dry hole. The senior leaders of the drug lab who were supposed to be there had left an hour before her team struck, but they'd left plenty of cartel troops in place.

The guy she'd hit raised his head to look at her with the twinned cyborg eyes of night-vision goggles. She heard the helo laboring as it struggled to pull back from the cliff. It went nose high—not a good sign.

And the MRZR began rolling backwards. She slammed it into first gear—with the engine stopped that should have been her parking brake. But the helo deck's angle was increasing and it wasn't enough. No chains in place yet to tie it to the deck.

"Out! Out! Out!" Tanya yelled at her crew.

First she stiff-armed Marta beside her, knocking her out of the passenger seat and onto the cargo deck. Then Tanya jumped out and pulled on Carl's shoulder to drag him out of the rear seat as Max jumped out the other side. Carl flopped down to the deck like a bag of steaming dogshit as the MRZR continued rolling backward. She snapped a monkey-line onto his vest's lifting ring so that he didn't slide away before she was ready to bandage him up.

"You gotta be kidding me!" The man she'd hit was being dragged by the vehicle as it continued rolling backward down the steeply slanted cargo bay. His foot was caught in the front bumper. A glance showed that the rear cargo ramp was still down, filled with yawning darkness.

She grabbed his hand, but it was too little-too late. In moments they were both sliding along the steel deck. Shouts followed them, but no hands were quick enough.

If she was being smart, she'd let go.

She wasn't being smart.

And his grip on her wrist was so powerful, it wouldn't matter if she did let go—because he didn't.

He kicked free of the MRZR just as they bumped over the rear ramp hinge. She almost got hold of a load tie-down ring, but their momentum ripped it out of her finger tips.

They were launched out of the rear of the helicopter, falling through the night, down into the dark shadows of the jungle-lined canyon.

Get Midnight Trust *at fine retailers everywhere.*
More information at: www.mlbuchman.com

ABOUT THE AUTHOR

M.L. Buchman started the first of, what is now over 50 novels and even more short stories, while flying from South Korea to ride his bicycle across the Australian Outback. All part of a solo around-the-world bicycle trip (a mid-life crisis on wheels) that ultimately launched his writing career.

Booklist has selected his military and firefighter series(es) as 3-time "Top 10 Romance of the Year." NPR and Barnes & Noble have named other titles "Best 5 Romance of the Year." In 2016 he was a finalist for RWA's prestigious RITA award.

He has flown and jumped out of airplanes, can single-hand a fifty-foot sailboat, and has designed and built two houses. In between writing, he also quilts. M. L. is constantly amazed at what you can do with a degree in Geophysics. He also writes: contemporary romance, thrillers, and fantasy.

More info and a free novel for subscribing to his newsletter at: www.mlbuchman.com

Join the conversation:
www.mlbuchman.com

Other works by M. L. Buchman:

The Night Stalkers
MAIN FLIGHT
The Night Is Mine
I Own the Dawn
Wait Until Dark
Take Over at Midnight
Light Up the Night
Bring On the Dusk
By Break of Day
WHITE HOUSE HOLIDAY
Daniel's Christmas
Frank's Independence Day
Peter's Christmas
Zachary's Christmas
Roy's Independence Day
Damien's Christmas
AND THE NAVY
Christmas at Steel Beach
Christmas at Peleliu Cove
5E
Target of the Heart
Target Lock on Love
Target of Mine

Firehawks
MAIN FLIGHT
Pure Heat
Full Blaze
Hot Point
Flash of Fire
Wild Fire
SMOKEJUMPERS
Wildfire at Dawn
Wildfire at Larch Creek
Wildfire on the Skagit

Delta Force
Target Engaged
Heart Strike
Wild Justice

White House Protection Force
Off the Leash
On Your Mark
In the Weeds

Where Dreams
Where Dreams are Born
Where Dreams Reside
Where Dreams Are of Christmas
Where Dreams Unfold
Where Dreams Are Written

Eagle Cove
Return to Eagle Cove
Recipe for Eagle Cove
Longing for Eagle Cove
Keepsake for Eagle Cove

Henderson's Ranch
Nathan's Big Sky
Big Sky, Loyal Heart

Love Abroad
Heart of the Cotswolds: England
Path of Love: Cinque Terre, Italy

Dead Chef Thrillers
Swap Out!
One Chef!
Two Chef!

Deities Anonymous
Cookbook from Hell: Reheated
Saviors 101

SF/F Titles
The Nara Reaction
Monk's Maze
the Me and Elsie Chronicles

Strategies for Success (NF)
Managing Your Inner Artist/Writer
Estate Planning for Authors

Made in the USA
Columbia, SC
01 October 2018